For Sue

First published in hardback in Great Britain by HarperCollins Children's Books in 2010

5 7 9 10 8 6 4

ISBN: 978-0-00-726384-4

Text and illustrations copyright © Oliver Jeffers 2010

HarperCollins Children's Books is a division of HarperCollins Publishers Ltd.

Visit our website at: www.harpercollins.co.uk

Printed in China

Up and Down

This WAY →

OLIVER JEFFERS

HarperCollins *Children's Books*

Once there were two friends...

and they always did
everything together.

Until one day the penguin decided there was something important he wanted to do all by himself...

...fly!

He did own wings after all,

even if they didn't work very well.

Although that didn't stop
the penguin from trying.

And trying.

But nothing worked,
and it wasn't long before
he ran out of ideas.

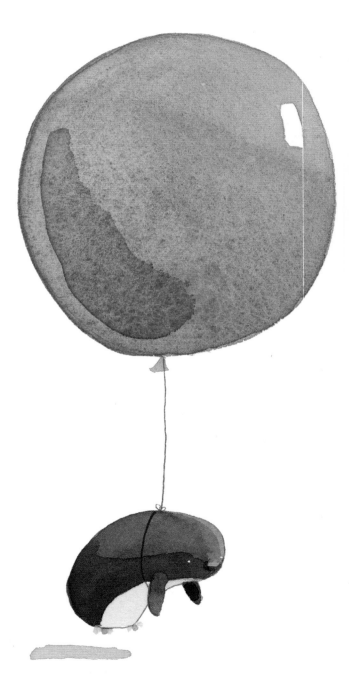

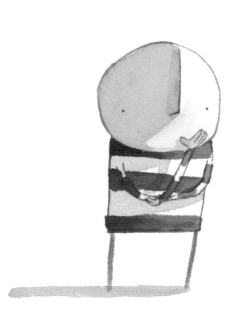

The boy even offered him a go
in his plane, but the engine hadn't
recovered from its last flight.

And besides, it wasn't the same.
The penguin wanted to do this by himself.

After doing a bit of homework,
it seemed as though the odds were
against him.

So together the boy and the penguin
decided it was time to ask for help...

EVER DREAMED
of FLYING ?

ARE YOU SHORT & FAT?

The TRAVELLING SHOW
IS LOOKING FOR A NEW
LIVING ☆
CANNON BALL

OWLS
→

NAR

when something
caught the penguin's eye
and he knew this was
his chance.

In his
excitement,
he rushed off
without a word.

The boy didn't know
where he had gone.

The boy looked everywhere,
and even thought he'd
found his friend
for a second.

Although none
of these other penguins
knew how to play his favourite game.

Meanwhile, the penguin had found the right place and was hired on the spot.

Soon he'd get to fly...

but suddenly, he realised
he didn't know where
his friend was or how
to get home.

Later that night,
the penguin couldn't
help but miss
his friend.

Likewise, the boy
could barely sleep
for worrying about
his friend.

The next day, the boy tried to think
of all the places the penguin would go,

when something caught his eye.
He didn't have much time.

The penguin's big moment had come but somehow he wasn't so sure about flying anymore.

He wished the boy were there and even
wondered if his friend had noticed he'd gone?

But it was too late for thoughts like that.

BAM!

He took off like a bullet!

The boy rushed in hoping he could still
catch his friend.

The penguin couldn't believe
how high and how fast he was flying,
and he had no idea how he was
going to land.

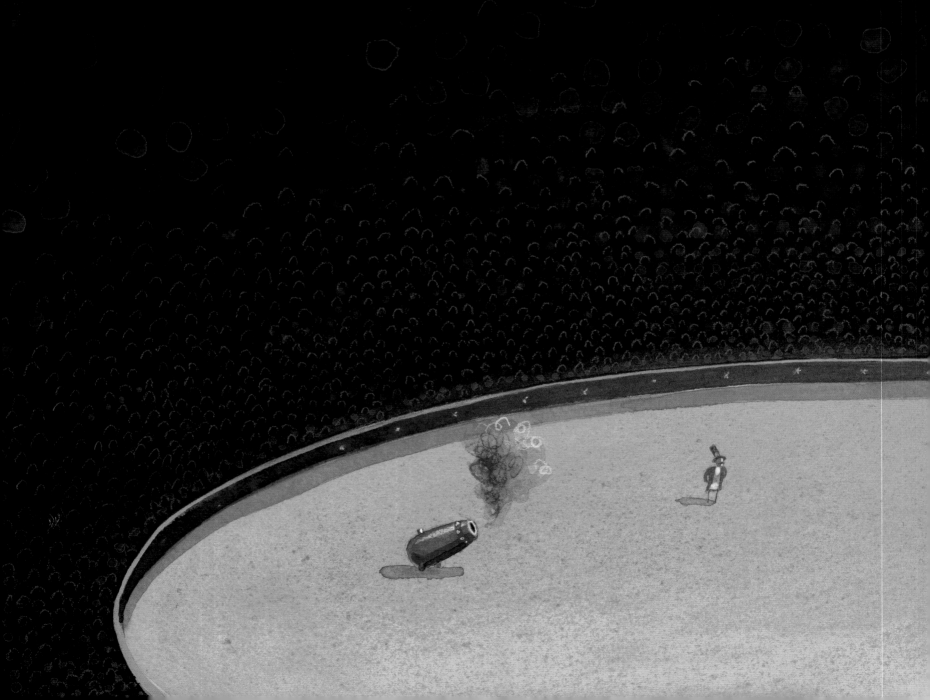

He was terrified and wished
his friend was there to help him.

The boy was there to catch him.

The friends agreed that there was a reason why his wings didn't work very well...

because penguins don't like flying.

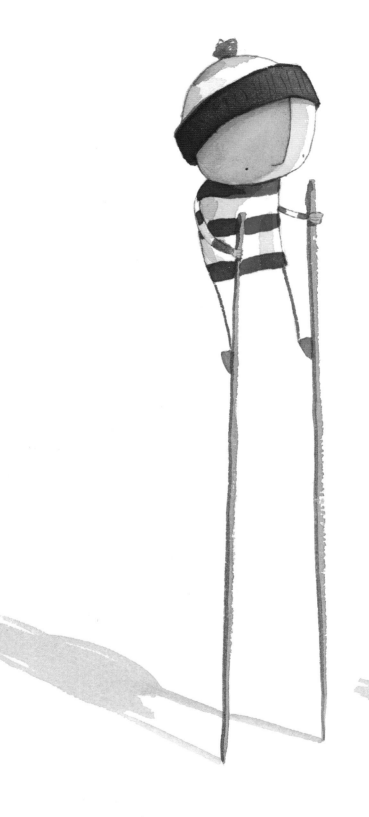

So together
the two friends
made a break
for home...

to play their favourite game.